D0281572

Stories adapted from the originals by Anne McKie.
Illustrations by Ken McKie.

Published by
GRANDREAMS LIMITED
Jadwin House, 205/211 Kentish Town Road,
London NW5 2JU.

Printed in Czechoslovakia.

ISBN 0 86227 897 X

YF5

Favourite tales
in this book
The Little Red Hen
The Enormous Turnip
The Sorcerer's
Apprentice
The Big Fat Pancake

THE LITTLE RED HEN

Once upon a time there was a Little Red Hen. She lived in a tiny house right at the bottom of a long bumpy country lane, with fields and meadows all around.

Now the Little Red Hen worked very hard and was always busy. All day long she cleaned and tidied her tiny house and worked by herself in the garden.

She clipped the hedges and weeded the paths; she grew beautiful flowers and lots of different vegetables. The Little Red Hen loved her garden, most of all she liked planting things and watching them grow.

On fine warm days bees and butterflies flew from flower to flower, and birds whistled all around her as she worked.

"Seeds to sow, lawns to mow, the cabbage patch to dig and hoe, and never a moment's rest!" the Little Red Hen sang to herself, as she scurried from one job to another.

Sometimes on warm afternoons, her friends from the farm at the top of the long bumpy lane, would come to visit her.

Whenever the Little Red Hen saw the Cat, the Rat and the Dog walking up her garden path, she would run inside to put on a clean apron. Then she would make a big jug of her homemade lemonade, fill a large tray with biscuits and slices of iced cake, and carry it out into the garden.

While the Little Red Hen was busy in the house, the Cat, the Rat and the Dog would stroll around her garden smelling the flowers. Each of them would then pick a huge bunch of the biggest and best to take home - without even asking the Little Red Hen!

Then the three friends would swing to and fro in the garden hammock, while the Little Red Hen served them lemonade and cake.

"We need a rest!" sighed the Rat. "It's a long walk from the farm, and we're all very tired!"

And with that, the Cat, the Rat and the Dog fell fast asleep - leaving the Little Red Hen to clear up!

Now right beside the Little Red Hen's house was a small field. One spring morning, as she looked out of her window, Little Red Hen had an idea. "I will ask the farmer for a sack of corn and plant my own field, then I shall have plenty of corn to grind into flour to make bread!"

As she hurried down the long bumpy lane to find the Farmer, the Little Red Hen said to herself, "I will ask my friends the Cat, the Rat and the Dog to help me, and together we will soon plant the field!"

The Farmer gladly gave the Little Red Hen a sack of his best corn. In return she gave him a pot of her homemade raspberry jelly and a basket full of ripe red cherries.

As she crossed the farmyard, the Little Red Hen spotted the Cat, the Rat and the Dog.

"Will you come and help me plant my field?" she called across to them.

"Not I!"
said the Cat.

"Not I!"
said the Rat.

"Not I!"
said the Dog,

and off they scurried.

"Then I shall do it myself!" said the Little Red Hen. And so she did.

So the Little Red Hen set to work. She planted her corn in long straight rows, one grain at a time.

It was hard work and very boring. However, the Little Red Hen kept on and on.

At last she stopped for lunch, but only for five minutes!

In the afternoon it began to rain, but the Little Red Hen went on planting grain after grain.

Very soon she was wet and her feet were covered with brown sticky mud, but she did not stop until the bag of grain was empty.

At last the whole field was planted and the Little Red Hen went inside.

In a short while the corn began to grow. If the Little Red Hen looked really hard, she could just see hundreds of soft green shoots peeping through the soil.

During the next few weeks the corn grew a bit taller every day.

As the long hot days of summer passed, the sun ripened the corn and turned it from green to gold. It was time for the Little Red Hen to cut the field.

Now who do you think should come visiting, but her friends the Cat, the Rat and the Dog.

"Will you help me cut my corn?" asked the Little Red Hen.

"I can't!" said the Cat.

"I can't!" said the Rat.

"I can't!" said the Dog, and they scampered away as quickly as they could.

"Then I shall cut it myself!" said the Little Red Hen. And so she did!

At the end of the day, Little Red Hen was dusty and tired, for all by herself she had gathered a whole field full of ripe corn.

Next day when the Little Red Hen opened the front door she saw her friends the Cat, the Rat and the Dog passing by.

"Will you help push my truck up the hill to the mill?" called the Little Red Hen.

"I won't!" said the Cat.

"I won't!" said the Rat.

"I won't!" said the Dog, and all three sat down on the grass for a rest.

"Then I shall take it myself!" said the Little Red Hen. And so she did!

So poor Little Red Hen had to push and pull the truck all the way along the long bumpy lane and up the hill to the mill.

"Come and sit down," said the Miller kindly, and he made her a cup of tea. "Rest here a while and I will grind your corn into flour!"

Feeling very hot and tired, the Little Red Hen sat on a bench and drank her tea. A gentle breeze blew the mill sails round and round and made Little Red Hen feel cool and fresh.

In a short while the huge stone wheels of the mill had ground the corn into flour. Then the Miller loaded the bags onto Little Red Hen's truck - to save her the trouble.

Going back home was easy for the Little Red Hen. The truck rolled so fast down the hill from the mill, it sped all the way down the long bumpy lane until it came to a stop - right outside Little Red Hen's front door.

"Tomorrow," said Little Red Hen, "I shall take some of my flour into town for the Baker to make into loaves of bread!" And off she went to bed.

Early next morning, the Little Red Hen loaded some of the bags of flour onto her wheelbarrow.

As she went out of her garden gate her three friends, the Cat, the Rat and the Dog passed by once more.

"Who will help me take my flour to the Baker?" asked the Little Red Hen.

"Not I!" said the Cat.

"Not I!" said the Rat.

"Not I!" said the Dog, and they strolled off in the opposite direction.

"Then I shall do it myself!" said the Little Red Hen. And so she did.

When she reached the bakery, the Baker was standing outside.

"Come in, Little Red Hen!" he shouted. "Help yourself to some of my pastries, while I bake your flour into bread."

So the Little Red Hen went into the Baker's shop. She sat behind the counter, nibbled her delicious pastry and chatted to the customers for a while.

The bread was ready at last. The Baker took it out of his big brick oven, and put all the loaves into the Little Red Hen's wheelbarrow ready for her to take home.

Can you guess who just happened to be standing outside the shop, sniffing the smell of freshly baked bread? It was the Cat, the Rat and the Dog.

The Little Red Hen wheeled the barrow full of loaves right up to the three friends.

"Now, who will help me eat my bread when I get home?" asked the Little Red Hen.

"I will!" cried the Cat.
"I will!" cried the Rat.
"And so will I!" cried the Dog.
"No you will not!" said the Little Red Hen with a smile. "I shall eat it myself!"

How the Baker's boy laughed. The Cat, the Rat and the Dog went away sulking, and the Little Red Hen turned back down the long bumpy lane and had fresh bread for her tea.

The very next day, Little Red Hen packed up three baskets of her finest vegetables and flowers from the garden. They were gifts for the Farmer, the Miller and the Baker who had been so kind and helpful to her.

As for the Cat, the Rat and the Dog, they got nothing - because that is all they deserved!

The Enormous Turnip

It was springtime in the valley and the farmer knew that the time was right to plant his seeds.

"What shall we plant in our field this year, my dear?" he called to his wife in the farmyard.

"Let me see!" said the farmer's wife. "Last year we planted beans, the year before it was corn, and before that we grew carrots."

Just at that moment their children came tumbling out of the barn. "Let's plant turnips this time!" they shouted.

And so they did!

The sun had just come out after a shower of rain, which made the soil warm and damp - just right for the turnip seeds.

Straightaway the whole family set to work. First the farmer harnessed up his horse and ploughed the ground.

Next the farmer's wife and all the children raked the soil until it was level, all the lumps were gone and it was soft and fine - just right for turnip seeds!

The farmer and his family worked very hard, and in next to no time every row was planted.

Carefully they covered up the seeds and made quite sure not a single one was showing, (as birds have very sharp eyes and love to gobble up turnip seeds).

Before they went back to the farmhouse the children made a scarecrow, just to make quite sure the birds wouldn't fly down and steal the freshly sown seeds.

The warm spring days soon passed, and by the end of the hot summer the little seeds had grown into large round turnips.

One day, as the farmer walked across the field, he spotted one turnip twice as big as the rest.

The next day when he crossed the field again, it was even bigger.

The farmer looked puzzled. "I must be dreaming!" he said to his dog. "I'm sure that turnip is growing bigger every minute!"

When the farmer's wife went into the field to look, the turnip had grown even more - it was almost as high as the scarecrow.

During the night the turnip grew bigger and bigger. By next morning the children could see it from the farmhouse windows. "Look at our Enormous Turnip!" they yelled with delight.

"Time we pulled it up!" the farmer told his wife at breakfast.

"How on earth are we going to do that?" gasped the woman, looking worried.

"If everybody lends a hand it will be easy!" nodded the farmer. And he went off to fetch a long rope from the barn.

The children thought this would be great fun, and happily went along to the field to help.

Carefully the farmer wound the rope right around the Enormous Turnip, and tied a tight knot at the front.

Then he wrapped the end of the rope round the middle and he pulled, and he pulled, and he pulled. But the Enormous Turnip never moved.

The farmer's wife stepped forward to help. She held on tight to the farmer and together they both pulled, and pulled, and they pulled. Still the Enormous Turnip did not move!

One by one the children joined in, until the whole family was pulling and tugging on the rope with all their might.

"All together now! One, two, three, pull!" yelled the farmer.

And pull they did. They pulled so hard, they all fell over laughing and squealing. And still the Enormous Turnip stayed right where it was!

By this time, some of the neighbours heard the noise and offered to help. Soon everyone was pulling on the rope, just like a tug-of-war team. Still the Enormous Turnip never moved.

"Well I never!" sighed the farmer shaking his head. And off he went to harness his horse.

So there they all were heaving and pulling - the horse, the neighbours, the children, the farmer's wife and the farmer. But it was no good. Nothing could move that Enormous Turnip.

The animals in the farmyard noticed the horse being lead into the turnip field, so they all followed, because they wanted to help too.

So here we have, the cat, the dog, the sheep, the goat, the cow, the horse, the neighbours, the children, the farmer's wife and the farmer - all trying to pull up that Enormous Turnip!

Just then a tiny fieldmouse scurried by. When he spied the end of the rope, he stopped and gave it a little tug.

Much to everyone's surprise, the Enormous Turnip popped right out of the ground. It rolled across the field and came to rest in the farmyard!

"Well I'll be blowed!" chuckled the farmer. "You're the strongest mouse I've ever met!"

After a while, when they had all calmed down, the farmer's wife took a picture.

"Smile please!" she said. But someone was not smiling. It was the farmer, who looked rather worried.

"What on earth are we going to do with the Enormous Turnip, now that we have pulled it up?" he asked them all.

"Take it to market of course!" cried the children.

But that was easier said than done.

First they tried to load it onto the wheelbarrow, but it was far too big.

Then they tried to load it onto the farmer's old truck. But the Enormous Turnip was so heavy, all the tyres burst.

So the farmer harnessed up his horse, and together everyone pushed and pulled the Enormous Turnip all the way to market. And the tiny fieldmouse came along to lend a hand as well!

The folks at the market were amazed when they saw the Enormous Turnip, and thay all rushed to buy some.

"There's plenty for everyone!" called the farmer, as he watched the Enormous Turnip being cut up into pieces.

At the market that day people bought nothing but turnip.

VEGETABLES
BEST BUY TODAY
-TURNIP
TURNIP FUDGE

And when it was time to go home every bit of the Enormous Turnip had been sold. So the farmer harnessed up his horse and they all headed for home.

The sun was going down as they reached the farmhouse, and the farmer asked his wife, "What shall we plant in the field next year?"

The farmer's wife turned to him and smiled. "Carrots, beans, barley, sweetcorn - anything but TURNIPS!"

Once upon a time, in the days when
Wizards were still casting spells,
and Witches still rode on broomsticks,
there lived a young boy who longed for
some adventure....
His name was Hugh.

THE SORCERER'S APPRENTICE

He lived with his mother in a tumble-down cottage by a stoney track that led over the mountain.

One morning, as Hugh was mending the cottage window, he happened to glance into the kitchen. There he saw his mother take down the money chest from the shelf, open up the lid and find - just one gold coin!

"This is all the money we have left!" said his mother sadly.

So there and then, Hugh made up his mind to go and seek his fortune.

"Do be careful," said his mother. "Try not to get your feet wet, and always wear dry socks."

The sun was shining and the birds were singing as Hugh kissed his mother goodbye, and set off down the stoney track that led over the mountain.

On and on the boy walked, until up ahead, he noticed a strange figure striding along the road.

As he came closer, Hugh saw that the man was a wizard. Can you believe that? A wizard! With a pointed hat and pointed shoes, and a cloak covered in stars. He even had a cat. Now this is what Hugh called an adventure.

The wizard smiled and held out his hand. "You look like a clever boy," he said. "I need a clever boy like you to help me with my magic spells."

Hugh's eyes opened wide.

The wizard went on. "Come and work for me, and I will pay you well and teach you all my magic."

Hugh's eyes opened even wider.

"For I am a Great and Powerful Sorcerer, and I need an apprentice."

"I thought you were a wizard," Hugh gasped.

"A wizard?" snapped the Sorcerer. "I am a thousand times more powerful than any old wizard. I am a SORCERER!"

Boldly Hugh stepped forward and held out his hand. "Then I shall be the Sorcerer's Apprentice!"

The Sorcerer led the way to the Palace high up the mountain. On the journey Hugh made friends with the cat. "I'm glad I've found a friend like you," whispered Hugh to the cat, for deep down he felt a bit afraid of the Sorcerer.

Once inside the Palace, Hugh soon forgot his fears, for everything looked so exciting.

"You can help me with my spells if you like," whispered the Sorcerer in Hugh's ear. And he handed the boy a cloak and a pointed hat - just like his own.

All that day they worked magic together until Hugh was tired out.

"What a wonderful day this has been," said Hugh to the cat, as he fell into bed in a room high up in a tower of the Palace. And the Sorcerer's cat settled down beside him.

Next morning there was a loud knocking on Hugh's door. It was the Sorcerer! In his hand he held a long list. "See that all these jobs are done before I return with my friend the Witch!" And off he strode.

Straight away Hugh pulled on his clothes and ran down the winding stairs. As he peeped out of the narrow window, he could see the Sorcerer and the Witch walking across the countryside - making mischief!

and what mischief they made....

When Hugh got downstairs he looked at the list in despair. "I'll never do all this work before the Sorcerer comes back!"

All at once the Sorcerer's cat jumped up onto the table, and sat purring on top of a big leather book.

"You clever cat!" cried Hugh with delight. "It's the Sorcerer's Big Book of Magic Spells. Now I can do everything before he returns."

Carefully Hugh opened the Big Book of Magic Spells and picked up a spare magic wand.

"Broom, come out of the corner and sweep the floor!" And lo and behold, the broom obeyed.

"Broom, fetch some water to wash the floor!" Off went the broom and came back with a bucket full of water, and poured it all over the floor.

Then the broom fetched another, then another and another. But of course, poor Hugh didn't know the MAGIC WORD that stops spells. So very soon he was up to his ankles in water and his socks were very wet. Sadly he remembered what his mother had said: "Try not to get your feet wet, and always wear dry socks." How he wished he was back at home now!

Very soon the water was up to his knees, and still the broom kept bringing more.

Suddenly there came a sound like thunder. The whole Palace began to shake and fireworks seemed to be flying round the room.

The Sorcerer had returned!

In a voice full of rage he shouted the MAGIC WORD. The broom stopped and every drop of water vanished!

Poor Hugh was left standing in the middle of the floor, still holding the Big Book of Magic Spells.

"Give me that book, boy!" yelled the angry Sorcerer.

"I will not!" cried Hugh, holding it tightly. "I heard you say the MAGIC WORD! Now I know it, I am as powerful as you."

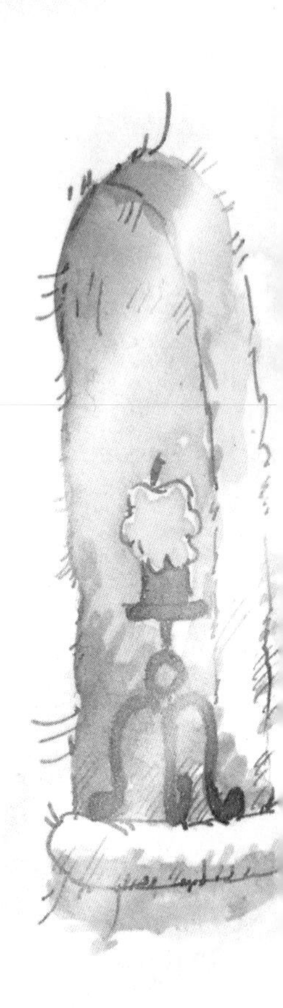

Furious with temper, the Sorcerer and the Witch tried every magic trick they could think of to outwit Hugh. But with the Big Book of Magic Spells and the MAGIC WORD, Hugh won every time.

Very soon the Sorcerer and the Witch were hopping up and down with rage.

Before they could stop him, Hugh grabbed the broom and whispered one of his spells.

The broom leapt across the room and began to beat the Sorcerer and the Witch very hard.

Away ran the wicked pair with the broom chasing after them. Out of the Palace they fled. Across the countryside and over the mountains until they disappeared from sight - never to be seen again!

As for Hugh, he went home to his loving mother and the Sorcerer's cat went with him.

They took the Big Book of Magic Spells and the MAGIC WORD, and always used them wisely.

They all lived happily ever after, and Hugh took great care never to get his socks wet again!

A Recipe for Pancakes

4oz plain flour, pinch of salt,
2 eggs, ½ pint of milk.

Sift flour and salt together in a bowl. Make a hollow in the centre with a wooden spoon, add the eggs and half the milk. Beat well until mixture is smooth, gradually add the rest of the milk to make a smooth creamy batter.

Melt a knob of butter in a frying pan, and pour in enough batter to thinly cover the base of the hot pan.

Fry until golden on the underside, then toss or flip with a palette knife, and cook on the other side.

THE BIG FAT PANCAKE

There was once a woman who had seven hungry children who just loved eating pancakes.

This kept the woman very busy at mealtimes. No sooner had she cooked a huge pile of crispy pancakes, than they all vanished. So she had to pick up her frying pan and start tossing pancakes, over and over and over again!

Her seven hungry children asked for pancakes for breakfast time, lunchtime, dinnertime, even at suppertime. In fact, they asked for pancakes whenever they felt hungry. So the woman had to pick up her frying pan and start tossing pancakes, over and over and over again!

To make matters worse, each one of the seven hungry children liked a different filling in their pancakes.

"I like maple syrup!" cried one.

"Honey and lemon for me!" said another.

"Mine's apple and brown sugar!" one shouted very loudly.

"Cherry sauce, chocolate chips, chopped nuts with a fudge topping!" gasped another.

"Blueberries and cream, please!" whispered the shy one politely.

"I like ham and cream cheese!" said the next-to-last.

"Cabbage!" nodded the very smallest child.

"Ugh! Cabbage!" cried all the rest.

So the woman picked up her frying pan and was just about to start tossing pancakes, over and over and over again, when she stopped.

"I've just had a wonderful idea!" she said smiling, as she put down the frying pan. "I will make one big fat pancake instead of lots of small ones. Why on earth didn't I think of it before?"

Her seven hungry children agreed this was a splendid idea and were all eager to help. So straight away they set to work.

Three of the bigger children ran off to find an extra large mixing bowl, and the other four quickly brought more flour, eggs, milk and butter.

Then all seven crowded round the kitchen table to watch their mother sift the flour into the bowl, make a well in the centre, and add the eggs.

They took it in turns to beat the mixture with a wooden spoon, then add the milk, a little at a time, to make a creamy batter.

"Oh, dear!" cried the woman, as she stared at the extra large mixing bowl full of batter. "My frying pan is too small to cook the big fat pancake!" The seven hungry children looked glum.

"How about that big shiny pan hanging up there?" cried the smallest child, and she pointed to a huge, round copper pan with a handle on either side.

"Perfect!" laughed the woman. "It's just the right size to cook the big fat pancake!"

How heavy the copper pan felt. It took every one of the seven hungry children to lift it up onto the stove.

At last everything was ready. In went the butter, sizzling and spitting as it melted in the hot pan. Next the creamy batter from the extra large mixing bowl was carefully poured in.

The big fat pancake sizzled and bubbled as it cooked, and a delicious smell filled the kitchen. Soon it curled around the edges and turned a lovely golden brown.

"Look at our beautiful big fat pancake!" cried the seven hungry children as they picked up their plates. "Let's eat it up at once!" and they waved their knives and forks in the air.

"Oh, no you don't!" yelled the Big Fat Pancake. "I'm far too clever to be eaten by anyone, for I am the Big Fat Pancake!"

With that, he hopped out of the copper pan, rolled across the kitchen floor, out of the cabin door and straight outside into the sunshine.

"Never before has anyone seen a pancake as big and as fat and as wonderful as me!" shouted the pancake as he bowled along.

Faster and faster he travelled with the seven hungry children chasing after him, yelling at him to stop.

On and on he sped, down village streets, past churches and little wooden houses, across gardens, under washing-lines and over bridges.

People stopped what they were doing and stared in amazement. Was that really a giant pancake that just rolled by?

"Take a good look at me!" yelled the pancake, pausing for a moment. "For I'm the famous Big Fat Pancake, the most wonderful pancake in the world!" Then off he sped.

Suddenly the seven hungry children ran past, trying to catch the pancake. And soon everyone had joined in the chase.

But the Big Fat Pancake was far too fast for all of them.

As he rolled quickly along the road, a big red rooster perched on a fence tried to peck a piece out of him.

When he whizzed down the hill, a flock of noisy black crows flew down to gobble him up - but the Big Fat Pancake was far too fast to be eaten by anyone!

Just for a second the pancake stopped and looked back. A long way behind him he could just see the village, a big red rooster and a flock of noisy black crows - all trying in vain to catch up with him.

Now this made the Big Fat Pancake laugh so much that he slipped through a wooden gate, right into a field full of pigs.

Some of the pigs were busy eating from their trough, while others were digging up the field with their pink snouts or rolling around in puddles of wet, sticky mud.

Only one of the pigs noticed the Big Fat Pancake. "Oink!" grunted the pig. "What a splendid pancake. Just the right size for my dinner!"

Now this pig was a very cunning pig, and had already thought of a clever plan to catch the tasty looking pancake.

At the edge of the pigs' field was a lake and the pancake was heading straight for the shore. As soon as he reached the water, the pancake remembered that he couldn't swim. So at last he had to stop.

Up trotted the pig and said in a kind, sweet voice: "Big Fat Pancake! Jump on my back and I will gladly take you across the lake!"

"What a pleasant, helpful pig you are!" replied the foolish pancake. And without a second thought, he jumped on the pig's back.

They had almost reached the other side when the pig tossed the Big Fat Pancake up onto his snout, and with a snap, he bit off a big piece of the pancake and swallowed it in one gulp.

With one mighty leap, the Big Fat Pancake just managed to reach the shore before the hungry pig could scramble out of the water.

By now, the seven hungry children, the people from the village, the red rooster, the flock of black crows and a few of the piglets, had chased all the way round the lake, and were standing on the shore.

"Stop at once, Big Fat Pancake!" they gasped (for they were all quite out of breath).

But the Big Fat Pancake was still too fast for them. Off he raced, over the hills and far away, shouting as he went, "No one can catch me! For I am the Biggest, Fastest Pancake in the whole wide world!" Then he disappeared from sight.

"That's the last we shall ever see of our delicious pancake," sighed the seven hungry children, who now felt even hungrier because of all the running and racing and chasing they had done following the Big Fat Pancake.

"Everyone must be starving after all that fresh air!" laughed the woman.

So it was decided there and then that they all go back to the cabin and have some pancakes.

Everyone helped, and everyone ate lots and lots of pancakes. The ones who had no idea how to make pancakes soon learned, it's very easy when you know how.

And if you see the pig, with his nose sniffing along the ground, you can be sure he's still searching for the Big Fat Pancake.